I0689011

Back From the Grave

"Some Secrets Never Die"

by

A. Abney

Preface

For the resilient women who have survived unimaginable hardship, and to those who have fought their way back from the depths of despair, your struggles have not gone unnoticed. To those who have found the strength to forgive—both themselves and others, I applaud you. It is a testament to the enduring power of the human spirit, its capacity for both profound darkness and radiant light. To the mothers who have loved fiercely, even when love felt impossible, and to the daughters who have sought understanding even when faced with profound rejection, this story is for you.

Further, this dedication extends to the countless women who have endured the silent suffering of domestic abuse, who have lived with the invisible wounds of betrayal and violence. Their courage in the face of adversity is a source of both inspiration and profound sorrow. May this story serve as a reminder that you are not alone, that your pain is valid, and that healing is possible, even in the face of unimaginable loss. May it also serve as a catalyst for conversations that need to be had, a call to action to break the cycle of violence and provide support for survivors. Finally, this dedication extends to anyone struggling with the profound grief of abandonment, whether it stems from the loss of a child, a partner, or a parent, recognizing the enduring scars that such experiences leave behind. May the strength and resilience found in these pages offer a glimmer of hope in the darkest of times. The path to healing is not easy but it is possible.

Contents

Chapter 1: The Breaking Point...........7

Chapter 2: The Search 53

Chapter 3: Redemption or Isolation?
.... 97

Chapter Four: The Beginning of the
End 151

Chapter Five: Tragedy 163

Chapter 1: The Breaking Point

The chipped paint on the windowsill mirrored the cracks forming in Angela's spirit. Sunlight, usually a source of warmth, felt harsh, emphasizing the dust mites dancing in the oppressive silence of their isolated apartment. Johnathan's absence was a familiar ache, replaced only by the heavier weight of his looming presence. He'd left again this time for "business," a euphemism that translated to days – sometimes weeks – spent in the smoky haze of bars, his laughter echoing back to her as a cruel mockery of her own despair. The silence, once a refuge, had become a suffocating blanket, woven with the threads of unspoken anxieties and festering resentments.

Initially, the abuse was subtle, a calculated erosion of her self-worth. A dismissive tone, a cold stare, a hand that lingered too long on her arm, transforming into a possessive squeeze that left bruises blooming beneath her sleeves. He'd call her names – useless, clumsy, pathetic – words that chipped away at her confidence until she felt less like a person and more like a broken doll, destined for his careless handling. She tried to rationalize it, to find excuses for his behavior. Stress, he said. Long hours, the pressure of meeting deadlines at work. She'd believe him, clinging to the remnants of the man she'd fallen in love with, the man who'd promised her the world, a life filled with laughter and sunshine, a life miles away from this isolated, claustrophobic existence.

The promises, however, were as brittle as the aging wood of their apartment floorboards. The laughter he'd spoken of was replaced by his drunken roars, his jeering insults cutting deeper than any physical blow. The sunshine was replaced by the shadows that crept into their home, lengthening with each passing day, each instance of his cruelty. Her attempts to escape, to reach out to her family, were met with threats, his possessive rage a tangible force that kept her trapped, ensnared in a web of fear and dependence. He controlled the finances, isolating her further, preventing her from seeking help. The phone calls to her sister, whispered into the dead of night, ended abruptly, silenced by the chilling sound of his footsteps approaching.

The apartment, initially a symbol of their shared dreams, became her prison. Her soul, once vibrant with life, felt empty and desolate, mirroring the barrenness of her own existence. The sounds of the neighborhood seemed to whisper warnings, a constant reminder of her vulnerability. She'd stare out the window, longing for escape, for the freedom of the open road, imagining a life beyond the confines of their four walls, a life where she wouldn't have to tremble at the sound of his key turning in the lock.

The escalating abuse became a chilling rhythm, a predictable pattern of escalating tensions, followed by apologies and fleeting moments of tenderness that only served to anchor her more firmly in her predicament. These were the moments that were designed to ensure her silence, a twisted form of emotional manipulation that trapped her in a cycle of hope and despair, rendering her unable to break free.

Then came the night that shattered her life completely. The memory remains vivid, a searing brand upon her soul, etching itself into the very fabric of her being. The darkness of the night, the chilling touch of the stranger, the invasion of her body, her spirit – it was a violation that transcended the physical, leaving her broken and shattered, her soul reduced to a wasteland of fear and self-loathing.

It wasn't the pain of the physical assault that haunted her the most, but the profound sense of helplessness, the crushing weight of her powerlessness. In the aftermath, she was left with a body scarred and a spirit broken, struggling to navigate the treacherous terrain of her violated reality, her sense of self brutally assaulted along with her body. The quiet screams echoing in her soul became a constant torment, a stark and unforgiving reminder of her vulnerability. The physical wounds would eventually heal, but the emotional scars would remain deep and unyielding.

The following weeks and months were a blur of emotional turmoil. The numbness that had initially served as a protective shield slowly began to crack, revealing the raw, unbearable pain that threatened to consume her. She was haunted by recurring nightmares, replaying the horrific events over and over again, unable to escape the clutches of the past. Sleep became a luxury, replaced by sleepless nights, filled with the incessant replay of the night's horror in her mind.

During the day, she moved through life like a ghost, detached and emotionally numb, her eyes vacant, her movements mechanical. The apartment, once her prison, now seemed alien and unwelcoming, a constant reminder of her traumatic experience. She found herself staring blankly at the walls, the once familiar objects appearing cold and lifeless. The vibrant colors of the apartment seemed to have been leached away, leaving behind only a stark and desolate landscape mirroring the turmoil raging within her. Even the simple act of eating had become a struggle. Her appetite had vanished, and the once nourishing food now seemed tasteless and devoid of substance.

The weight of her secret grew heavier with each passing day. The fear of Johnathan's reaction if she were to confide in him, or anyone

else for that matter, served to ensure
her continued silence. Her loneliness
was intensified by her inability to
reach out to family and friends, her
isolation a self-imposed prison born
from fear and despair.

Then came the cruelest blow of all.
The doctor's visit, the confirmation
of an unwanted pregnancy, the
stark, sterile white of the examining
room amplifying her feelings of
revulsion and despair. The news hit
her like a physical blow, a crushing
weight adding to the burden she
already carried. The life growing
within her served only as a constant
reminder of the violence, of the
violation that had occurred and her
powerlessness in the face of it. This
pregnancy was not a symbol of hope
or new beginnings, but instead, a
physical manifestation of her pain, a
living testament to her violation. It
was in that moment, amid the sterile

scent of antiseptic, that she felt truly alone and utterly broken. She thought to herself, "how am I going to raise another child?"

And then came the ultimate betrayal, the revelation of Johnathan's infidelity, his casual admission of another woman, another life he was creating outside their increasingly broken union. His casual disclosure left Angela reeling, an additional layer of pain added to the already overwhelming weight of her trauma. It solidified her sense of worthlessness, reinforcing her conviction that she was nothing more than a discarded object. His words were not merely a betrayal of their marriage, but a callous dismissal of her very being.

The cumulative weight of it all—the abuse, the rape, the pregnancy, and Johnathan's callous infidelity—pushed Angela to the brink. Her sense of self had been completely eroded; she felt utterly alone, utterly defeated. The choice she made, born of desperation, fear and a profound sense of worthlessness, was a tragic consequence of her circumstances, a terrible act born of trauma. It was a decision she would live to regret for the remainder of her life. The decision to abandon her child to the sterile environment of a hospital, a cold, uncaring institution; the decision to give up her daughter for adoption; the act of severing the umbilical cord of her motherhood; the false report of her daughter's death, it was a chilling act that would have far-reaching and devastating consequences. But in that moment, amidst the turmoil and despair, it felt like the only option, the only way to escape the suffocating darkness that had enveloped her existence.

The sterile white of the doctor's office felt like a tomb. The antiseptic smell, usually meant to convey cleanliness and safety, only amplified Angela's feelings of revulsion and despair. The doctor's words, delivered with professional detachment, echoed in the oppressive silence: "You're pregnant, Mrs. Carter." The confirmation hung in the air, heavy and suffocating, a physical weight pressing down on her already shattered spirit. She stared blankly at the sterile, stainless steel instruments, their gleaming surfaces reflecting her own pale, drawn face. It wasn't the physical reality of the pregnancy that appalled her; it was the source, the brutal violation that had birthed this new life, twisting a potential miracle into a constant, agonizing reminder of her powerlessness.

This wasn't the joyous announcement she had once imagined, the moment of profound connection between mother and child. This pregnancy was a cruel mockery, a grotesque symbol of her violated body and spirit. It was a living testament to the night her sense of self were stolen. The life growing inside her wasn't a source of hope or anticipation; it was a constant, visceral reminder of her trauma, a living embodiment of her pain and vulnerability. Her hands trembled, clutching the worn fabric of her skirt as if seeking some small measure of comfort, some shred of normalcy in the chaos swirling within her.

The doctor's gentle attempts at reassurance felt hollow, meaningless in the face of her overwhelming despair. Her mind raced, a whirlwind of fear and uncertainty.

She couldn't even bring herself to consider the future, to contemplate the implications of this pregnancy, the very idea felt like an insurmountable weight, a crushing burden added to the already unbearable load she carried. The future stretched ahead, a bleak and unforgiving landscape of uncertainty.

Leaving the doctor's office felt like stepping back into a nightmare. The bright sunlight, usually a welcome sight, felt harsh and unforgiving, exposing the fragility of her soul. She wandered aimlessly, her legs carrying her through the familiar landscape of her life, a life that now felt both utterly foreign and hopelessly inescapable. Each step was a laborious effort, a testament to the profound emotional exhaustion that had taken root within her.

Then, the shattering blow. Johnathan's confession. Not a tearful apology, not a plea for forgiveness, but a casual, almost careless admission. "There's someone else, Angela," he'd said, the words dripping with a casual cruelty that cut deeper than any physical blow. He hadn't just betrayed their marriage; he'd betrayed her very sense of self, her dignity, her worth. And then the final, sickening twist: she was pregnant, too. Another woman, another child, another life he was creating, completely oblivious to the devastation he was leaving in his wake. It was as if he hadn't just rejected her; he'd erased her entirely, rendering her existence inconsequential, meaningless.

The revelation of his infidelity was not simply a betrayal, it was the ultimate validation of her own feelings of worthlessness, the

confirmation of her fear that she was
nothing more than a discarded
object. His callous admission served
only to amplify her feelings of
isolation, intensifying her sense of
being completely alone and utterly
defeated. The weight of her
unspoken sorrow felt
overwhelming, almost unbearable.

The news shattered the last vestiges
of her fragile hope, leaving her in a
state of profound emotional
devastation. It wasn't simply the
betrayal of her husband; it was the
shattering of her already fragile
sense of self, the complete erosion of
her worth and dignity.

The days and nights that followed
were a blur of fragmented memories
and emotional chaos. Sleep offered
no escape, replaced by a relentless
cycle of nightmares, the horrors of
the night replaying themselves
relentlessly in her mind. She found

herself wandering through the house like a ghost, detached and emotionally numb. The apartment, once her prison, had become a symbol of her complete desolation.

The once vibrant colors of her home seemed leached away, replaced by a cold, sterile pallor, mirroring the turmoil raging within her. The familiar objects held no comfort, the mundane routines felt burdensome and meaningless. Even the simple act of caring for her two young children felt like an unbearable burden, her capacity for love and nurturing depleted.

The escalating despair and isolation began to take its toll. She lost her appetite, the nourishing food once enjoyed now tasteless and unappetizing. Her body, once strong and vibrant, was now emaciated, reflecting the emotional starvation she was experiencing. Her once bright eyes were now vacant and dull, reflecting the emptiness within her soul. Her thoughts were consumed by a dark and unrelenting despair, each passing moment dragging her deeper into the abyss of hopelessness.

The weight of her secret, the unwanted pregnancy, and the devastating revelation of Johnathan's infidelity became an unbearable burden. The shame and guilt were crushing, making her withdraw further into herself. She was trapped in a cycle of self-loathing and despair, her sense of self-worth completely eroded. The world around her seemed to fade, her life reduced to a desolate landscape mirroring the emptiness within.

The maternal instincts she had once
cherished flickered weakly against
the overwhelming weight of her
trauma. The conflicting emotions
created a vortex of turmoil within
her; the pull of motherhood, the
natural desire to nurture and protect
her unborn child, battled against the
profound revulsion she felt toward
the pregnancy and the man who had
fathered it. Her decision, born of
profound despair and a desperate
need to escape the unbearable pain,
was tragically flawed, yet utterly
comprehensible in the context of her
overwhelming circumstances.

The prospect of raising a child
fathered through such violence felt
unbearable. The thought of facing
the world with the stigma of her
violation was a crushing weight, a
burden too heavy to contemplate.
The image of the child, a physical
manifestation of the trauma, only

served to intensify her feelings of despair, leaving her feeling trapped and utterly hopeless. Her decision was born not of malice, but of a desperate attempt to escape the relentless cycle of pain, violence, and betrayal that had defined her life. It was a decision fueled by desperation, a desperate bid to salvage something of herself from the wreckage of her life, but a decision that would follow her, haunt her, and shape the remainder of her existence.

The fluorescent lights of the hospital hallway hummed a relentless, sterile counterpoint to the chaotic storm raging inside Angela. Each step felt leaden, each breath shallow, as if the very air itself weighed her down. The antiseptic scent, meant to be reassuring, only served to amplify her sense of alienation, of being adrift in a sea of cold, uncaring efficiency. The hospital, a place meant for healing, felt like a mausoleum, a stark and impersonal setting for the agonizing decision she was about to make.

She clutched the worn, floral-patterned handbag close to her chest, its familiar texture the only shred of comfort in this desolate landscape. Inside, nestled amongst crumpled tissues and a half-empty pack of cigarettes, lay the tiny, hand-knitted booties – a cruel reminder of the life she was about to relinquish. The booties, painstakingly crafted in stolen moments of quiet desperation, represented a love she couldn't afford to feel, a motherhood she couldn't afford to embrace.

Her reflection in the polished steel of the water fountain showed a gaunt, hollowed-out version of herself – a woman barely recognizable as the vibrant, hopeful young woman she once was. Dark circles ringed eyes that had lost their sparkle, their depths filled with a sorrow so profound it felt physical. Her face, etched with lines of worry and fatigue, revealed years of silently born pain, a lifetime of unspoken trauma. The pale skin was stretched taut over her bones, her body mirroring the emotional starvation she'd endured.

She told herself it was for the best, a mantra whispered repeatedly in the quiet spaces between her ragged breaths.

It's for Jessica's sake, she'd reason, clinging to the flimsy rationale as if it were a lifeline. *She deserves a better life, a life I can't give her.* But even as she repeated the words, the hollowness of her justifications echoed back, exposing the profound self-deception that fueled her desperate act.

The truth was far more complicated, far more tangled in the thorns of her own self-hatred and the unrelenting burden of her past. This wasn't merely a selfless act of sacrifice; it was a desperate attempt to escape her own unbearable pain, a brutal act of self-preservation cloaked in the guise of altruism.

The nurse, a woman with kind eyes and a weary demeanor, appeared at the door, her expression a mixture of professional detachment and quiet compassion. Angela followed the nurse, her steps slow and deliberate, each one dragging her further into the heart of her agonizing decision. The room was small, sparsely furnished, with the cold, clinical sterility that characterized the entire hospital. A small bassinet sat next to a steel table, gleaming under the harsh fluorescent lights, a silent witness to the drama unfolding.

Inside the bassinet lay Jessica, swathed in a soft, pink blanket. Angela's breath caught in her throat as she gazed at her daughter, a tiny, perfect being completely unaware of the fate that awaited her. The infant's soft, rosy skin, her tiny fingers curled into fists, her gentle breathing, all served as a painful reminder of the innocence she was about to shatter.

She approached cautiously, her hands trembling as she reached out to touch Jessica's cheek. The infant's skin was soft and warm against her fingertips, a stark contrast to the icy chill of the room. A wave of emotion washed over Angela – a tsunami of love, guilt, and profound despair. She wanted to hold her daughter close, to feel the warmth of her body against her own, to feel the comfort of her closeness. But the reality of her circumstances, the inescapable weight of her own trauma, held her back.

The rationalizations, carefully constructed over weeks of agonizing internal debate, threatened to crumble. The fear, the crushing weight of responsibility, the overwhelming sense of inadequacy—they all clawed at her, threatening to drown her in a sea of regret. The nurses' gentle encouragement felt like a distant hum, a background noise to the deafening roar of her own inner turmoil.

She whispered a silent prayer, a desperate plea for forgiveness, even as she knew the act she was about to commit would be unforgivable. She couldn't bear the thought of her daughter growing up in the shadow of her abusive marriage, of carrying the weight of her mother's trauma. This, she told herself, was the

ultimate act of love. The ultimate
sacrifice.

With a trembling hand, she signed
the adoption papers, each signature
a nail hammered into the coffin of
her motherhood, each stroke a
betrayal of her own heart. The act
was both swift and agonizingly
slow, her entire being screaming in
protest even as her hand moved
mechanically across the page.

The false death report felt like a final
betrayal, a callous lie that she
justified as a necessary evil. The
official-sounding words, meant to
create a semblance of closure, only
served to underscore the finality of
her choice, confirming the
devastating reality of her
abandonment.

She left the hospital numb, drained,
hollowed out. The world outside
seemed unreal, muted, as if viewed

through a hazy filter of disbelief. The vibrant colors of the autumn leaves seemed strangely out of place, their beauty a cruel mockery of the desolation in her heart.

The ensuing weeks and months were a blur of forced normalcy. She returned to her routine, taking care of her sons, pretending that nothing had changed. She avoided mirrors, her face a landscape of unspoken grief. She found solace in the relentless routine, allowing it to distract her from the overwhelming emptiness that consumed her. But the image of Jessica, her sweet, innocent face, haunted her waking moments and plagued her sleep. The emptiness gnawed at her, a constant reminder of the choice she'd made, a choice that would forever shape her identity, her relationships, and the very essence of her being. The silence in her heart, once a sanctuary

from the torment, had now become
a deafening roar, a constant
reminder of the life she had chosen
to relinquish, a life that would
forever remain a painful, unfillable
void.

The lie became a part of her, a
suffocating shroud that wrapped
itself around her heart, stealing
away her joy, her hope, and any
semblance of inner peace. Every
smile she gave felt like a betrayal,
every moment of happiness a fragile
façade masking the crushing weight
of her secret. Twenty-five years she
carried this burden, a silent prisoner
of her own creation. The weight of
her decision, the guilt and self-
loathing, remained a constant
companion, a relentless tormentor
whispering doubts and
condemnations in the silent spaces
of her heart.

The train rattled, a rhythmic counterpoint to the relentless drumming of guilt in Angela's chest. She stared out the rain-streaked window, the blurring landscape mirroring the chaos within. Leaving the hospital had felt like escaping a suffocating nightmare, but the relief was fleeting, replaced by a gnawing emptiness that clung to her like a second skin. She'd chosen a new life, a new city, a new identity—all meticulously constructed to distance herself from the wreckage of her past. But the past, it seemed, had a way of traveling with you, no matter how far you ran.

The apartment she'd chosen was small, functional, devoid of warmth or personality. It reflected her emotional state—bare, sterile, a refuge from the world rather than a home. There were no photographs on the walls, no trinkets or mementos to personalize the space. Everything was clean, minimal, almost clinical. It felt safe, a protective shell against the vulnerability she so desperately tried to suppress. But the silence was deafening, a constant reminder of the void she'd created in her life.

The years that followed were a blur of routine, a carefully orchestrated performance of normalcy. She worked diligently, her efficiency and focus bordering on obsessive. Her sons, Mark and Michael, were her focus, her anchors in the turbulent sea of her own making. She showered them with a love that bordered on suffocating, a desperate attempt to atone for the emptiness she'd left in Jessica's life, to fill the hole in her own heart with the warmth of their presence. Yet, even their love, so freely given, could not completely penetrate the icy wall she'd built around her emotions.

Her relationship with Mark and Michael was complex, marked by both profound love and a subtle undercurrent of unease. She was a protective, almost overbearing mother, hovering over them, anticipating their needs before they were even voiced. This hyper-vigilance stemmed from a deep-seated fear—a fear of losing them, of repeating the unimaginable pain of abandonment. Her boys sensed this tension, this unspoken sadness that clung to her like a shadow. They loved her fiercely, but they also knew there was a part of her that remained inaccessible, a hidden chamber locked tight against the world.

Her own emotional life was a barren wasteland. She had no close friends, no confidantes to share her burden. The idea of intimacy, of vulnerability, felt terrifying. She'd experienced intimacy in the most destructive of ways, and the wounds from that experience ran deep. Trust felt like a luxury she could no longer afford. The men she dated were fleeting encounters, devoid of genuine connection. She kept them at arm's length, guarding her heart against the pain of further betrayal. Their attempts at emotional intimacy were met with coldness, with an emotional distance that left them bewildered and frustrated. She was a ghost, haunting the fringes of their lives, leaving before any genuine bond could be formed.

The silence surrounding Jessica's absence was a heavy shroud, suffocating her in its suffocating grip. She avoided all reminders of her—no photographs, no baby clothes, no mementos that might puncture the carefully constructed wall she'd erected around her grief. She never spoke of Jessica, not even to herself, her silence a testament to the depth of her guilt and self-loathing. The lie she had perpetuated—the fabricated death certificate—became an albatross around her neck, weighing down every action, every decision. The years accumulated, each one adding another layer of guilt and regret. The weight of her secret threatened to crush her, leaving her gasping for air in the suffocating darkness.

Her work became an escape, a relentless pursuit of efficiency and order. She threw herself into her career, finding solace in the structure and predictability of her job. It provided a necessary distraction, a shield against the relentless onslaught of her memories. But even her success felt hollow, a pyrrhic victory in the face of her inner turmoil. The accolades, the recognition, were meaningless without the inner peace she so desperately craved.

Sleep offered little respite. Her dreams were a chaotic tapestry of fragmented images—the brutal violence of her marriage, the sterile coldness of the hospital, the innocent face of Jessica, her eyes wide and unknowing. She'd wake up in a cold sweat, her heart pounding, the silence of the apartment amplifying her despair. The pills prescribed to help her sleep became a crutch, a temporary escape from the agonizing reality of her life. The fleeting numbness they offered was a small price to pay for the respite

from the relentless torrent of guilt
and regret.

The holidays were the worst. The
festive cheer of others only
highlighted the emptiness in her
own life. The family gatherings,
once filled with laughter and joy,
now felt like a painful reminder of
everything she'd lost—everything
she'd thrown away. She would
retreat into herself, creating an
impenetrable wall between her and
the warmth radiating from the
family dynamics around her. She
envied, with a silent, aching sadness,
the families she observed from
afar—families untouched by the
darkness that had consumed her.

Years bled into decades, each one a
testament to her self-imposed
isolation. The woman she was before
the abuse, the vibrant, hopeful
young woman, felt like a distant
memory, a ghost from a life she

could barely recall. Her reflection in the mirror showed a woman aged beyond her years, her eyes haunted, her face etched with the silent scars of her past. The outward appearance of normalcy masked a deep-seated unhappiness, a perpetual state of emotional starvation. She was a hollow shell, her life a testament to the devastating power of trauma, a silent testament to the enduring weight of her choice. The silence, once a refuge, had become a prison, a suffocating reminder of the life she'd abandoned, the daughter she'd given away, and the potential for a love she'd never allow herself to feel. The weight of her secret, once a manageable burden, had become an insurmountable mountain, threatening to bury her under its crushing weight. The possibility of redemption, once a distant glimmer of hope, now seemed impossible, lost in the suffocating darkness of her self-imposed exile.

The chipped porcelain mug warmed Angela's hands, the lukewarm tea doing little to soothe the chill that settled deep in her bones, a chill that had nothing to do with the November air. She sat by the window of her small apartment, the city lights a blurry tapestry against the darkening sky. Twenty-five years. Twenty-five years she'd lived with the lie, the gnawing guilt a constant companion. She'd built a life, a carefully constructed façade of normalcy, but the foundation was built on sand. One gust of wind, one unexpected encounter, and the whole thing could crumble.

Her coping mechanism, she realized with a bitter laugh, was avoidance. A meticulous, almost obsessive avoidance of anything that might trigger the raw, searing pain of her past. She had meticulously erased Jessica from her life, from her mind. There were no photographs, no baby clothes, no keepsakes to remind her of the daughter she'd abandoned. The silence surrounding Jessica's absence was a shield, a self-imposed exile that had become both a prison and a sanctuary.

Her relationship with her sons, Mark and Michael, was a tapestry woven with threads of love and fear. She loved them fiercely, showering them with affection and attention, smothering them, perhaps, in a desperate attempt to compensate for the emptiness she'd created in Jessica's life. It was a warped kind of atonement, a twisted attempt to purchase peace of mind through excessive devotion.

Mark, the elder son, was a replica of Johnathan, his dark hair and brooding eyes a constant reminder of the man who had inflicted so much pain. Seeing Mark's resemblance to his abusive father stirred a mixture of fear and loathing within Angela. She found herself becoming overly critical of Mark, and overprotective of Michael.

Michael, on the other hand, was the antithesis of his father. Quiet and thoughtful, he possessed an intuitive understanding of his mother's hidden pain. He saw the haunted look in her eyes, the tremor in her hands, the way she flinched at unexpected noises. He loved her unconditionally, but his love was laced with a poignant understanding of her emotional distance. He often tried to engage her in conversation about her past but was consistently rebuffed. He would leave silent offerings of his affection at her feet; a hand-drawn picture, a small gift, or a heartfelt hug.

Her work became an escape, a refuge from the relentless weight of her guilt. She had climbed the corporate ladder with ruthless efficiency, her focus bordering on obsessive. The accolades, the promotions, were hollow victories, a testament to her ambition but not to her happiness. Success provided a temporary distraction from the ever-present torment of her past. She poured all her energy into her work, finding solace in the structure and predictability of her career.

Weekends were often spent lost in cleaning. Every surface in her house was spotless, the floors gleamed under the harsh fluorescent lights. Every item was in its place. The act of cleaning and organising became her ritual of self-flagellation, an attempt to regain control over some aspect of her life.

Evenings were often spent lost in a haze of television shows that she barely watched. The mundane rhythm of the television show served to distract her from the more pressing pain within her own mind. She would lose herself for hours in the stories of fictional characters who did not have to carry her secrets.

She avoided intimacy like the plague, fearing that any connection, any vulnerability, would expose the fragile underpinnings of her carefully constructed life. Her dating life consisted of brief, superficial encounters, relationships built on avoidance rather than connection. Men came and went, their attempts at closeness met with a frosty reserve, a wall of silence that repelled any attempt at genuine intimacy.

Her self-destructive behavior manifested in different ways. The excessive working hours were one, but she also turned to alcohol occasionally, using it to numb the pain, to silence the relentless accusations of her conscience. The brief respite offered by alcohol was a poor exchange for the lingering hangover of guilt and regret that followed.

The few friends she had gradually drifted away, unable to penetrate the emotional distance she maintained. Their concern and empathy, however well-intentioned, were met with cold politeness, a carefully crafted detachment that kept them at arm's length.

Angela's self-image was shattered. She saw herself not as a mother, but as an abuser, a liar, an abandonment artist. She was a failure, a woman unworthy of love or forgiveness. The reflection staring back at her from the mirror was a stranger, a woman etched with the invisible scars of her past traumas. The vibrant, hopeful young woman she once was was a distant memory, a phantom from a life she could barely recall.

The city she lived in, once a symbol of escape, had become a cage. Every street corner, every building, every passing face held the potential for discovery, for exposure. The anonymity she sought was an illusion, her secret a weight she carried everywhere she went. The vibrant cityscape offered no solace, the vastness of it only emphasising her utter aloneness. The very

anonymity that had once been a
source of comfort became a source of
unease, the lack of personal contact
highlighting the distance she had
placed between herself and all
human connection.

The past wasn't simply a collection
of events; it was a living, breathing
entity, a shadow that followed her
everywhere, whispering accusations
in her ear. The silence she cultivated
was not peaceful; it was a
suffocating tomb, a self-built prison
that confined her to a life of
perpetual loneliness and remorse.
The memories—the brutal rapes, the
suffocating control, the bitter taste of
betrayal—came to haunt her with
terrifying clarity. The hospital,
where she'd given birth alone and
abandoned Jessica, became a symbol
of her deepest regret, a place she
could never revisit.

The train journey, a frequent escape
into the anonymity of the vast
network, had become a metaphor
for her life—a constant motion, a
perpetual state of transit, never truly
arriving, never finding rest. The
fleeting views outside the train's
window seemed to taunt her; idyllic
scenes of family life and happiness,
scenes which were permanently
inaccessible to her. The rhythmic
clatter of the train, once a soothing
backdrop, was now a relentless
reminder of her own inner turmoil.

And then, one day, a letter arrived.
A simple, unassuming envelope
bearing a return address from a
town she had never heard of. It
contained a single photograph, a
young woman with eyes that
mirrored her own. The shadow of
the past, it seemed, was finally about
to cast its long reach into the
present, shattering the fragile

illusion of normalcy she had so painstakingly constructed. The letter, a simple invitation to meet, had broken through her carefully constructed walls. The carefully manicured facade of her life was about to crumble, leaving her exposed, vulnerable, and facing the consequences of her past choices. The possibility of redemption was within reach, but the path was fraught with danger and uncertainty. The weight of twenty-five years of self-imposed exile would have to be faced.

Chapter 2: The Search

Jessica traced the faded floral pattern on the worn cotton sheets, the familiar texture a small comfort in the vast emptiness she felt. Twenty-five years. Twenty-five years she'd lived in a house filled with laughter and love, a life meticulously crafted by loving, if somewhat bewildered, adoptive parents. Yet, a persistent ache remained, a hollow space in her heart that no amount of affection could fill. It was a feeling she couldn't quite articulate, a sense of incompleteness, a missing piece of a puzzle she didn't even know existed.

Her childhood was idyllic, a tapestry woven with threads of warmth and security. The Doziers, her adoptive parents, were everything a child could hope for: kind, patient, and endlessly loving. They'd never pressured her to ask about her birth parents, understanding that the unknown might be more comforting than a potentially painful truth. They'd shielded her from any unnecessary turmoil, prioritizing her happiness above all else. She had two older brothers, Tom and David, who were like the protective bulwarks of her happy life. They treated her with affection and often got into playful scuffles with her, solidifying her family unit.

But even amidst the unwavering love and support of her family, a nagging question lingered, a faint echo in the back of her mind. It wasn't a conscious yearning for her biological parents; it was more of a subtle dissonance, a feeling of being slightly out of sync, a sense that some essential part of herself remained hidden, veiled in mystery.

She was a patchwork quilt of traits –
her mother's hazel eyes, her father's
stubborn chin, yet she couldn't quite
reconcile with her family. She felt a
connection to her adoptive family
that ran deep, but she was aware of
a vague feeling of disconnect, too.

The dissonance intensified as she
grew older, transitioning from the
carefree innocence of childhood to
the self-discovery of adolescence.
She excelled academically, her sharp
intellect and artistic talents setting
her apart. But her achievements felt
hollow, accomplishments detached
from a sense of true belonging. She
found herself analyzing family
portraits, searching for a hint of
resemblance, a subtle connection to
the unknown past. She'd stare at
photographs for hours, hoping to
find a clue about where she came
from.

Her artistic pursuits became an outlet for the undefined yearning within her. She poured her emotions onto canvases, painting vibrant, chaotic landscapes that mirrored the turmoil in her soul. Her art was bold, emotional, reflecting her inner struggle and seeking answers to the questions she dare not ask. Her creations often reflected the turbulent emotional landscape that lay within, a desperate search for meaning and connection.

It wasn't until her mid-twenties, during a particularly introspective period, that the subtle unease transformed into a driving force. A chance encounter with an elderly woman who'd been through adoption ignited a curiosity within her. The woman's stories of reunion, both joyful and heartbreaking, resonated deeply. The story of the elderly woman awakened a determination within Jessica, a determination that changed her course forever.

Armed with determination, Jessica began her search. It wasn't easy. Adoption records are often sealed, providing a veil of secrecy over what should have been a transparent process. But Jessica was persistent, relentless in her pursuit of the truth. She spent countless hours poring over documents, scouring databases, and contacting adoption agencies. She travelled to local county offices, and libraries – armed with nothing more than a few vague details from her adoption files. The process was frustrating, the lead's she chased often ended up in dead ends.

The trail was cold, the details scarce. She had only a few fragments – a vague birth date, the knowledge that she was abandoned shortly after birth in an unnamed town, along with a description of her birth mother, something akin to a mental snapshot given by an official at the orphanage. This vague description served as her compass, leading her through the maze of bureaucratic red tape. This was far more difficult than she'd imagined.

During this period, her adoptive family was both supportive and worried. They noticed her obsessive search and the quiet desperation that accompanied it. They understood her search, but were also concerned that she would find something painful and shattering. Her brothers, Tom and David, offered unwavering support, reminding her that she was loved, that her search didn't diminish their affection. But they also worried about what she might uncover.

Jessica's pursuit became all-consuming, a relentless journey that eclipsed all other aspects of her life. She put her artistic career on hold, sacrificing her creative pursuits for the sake of this quest for her identity. The search demanded every ounce of her energy, her focus unwavering in its intensity. The relentless pursuit became her sole preoccupation, eclipsing all other aspects of her life, her focus resolute and unwavering.

Slowly, painstakingly, she began to piece together the puzzle. A cryptic entry in a hospital ledger, a mention of a name in an old newspaper article, a faded photograph that resembled her—each clue was a small victory, a steppingstone on a long and arduous path. With each small piece of information, her determination grew. She was closer to her roots now, but as she got

closer, she felt a strange mix of
trepidation and excitement. She felt
prepared for anything. Or so she
thought.

Finally, after months of relentless
searching, she found it. A name. An
address. Angela. A name that
resonated with a power she didn't
understand, a name that echoed in
the silent spaces of her past. The
address led her to a small town, far
removed from her own life, a place
that held the key to unlocking her
past, to uncovering the mystery of
her origins. It was a leap of faith, a
decision fraught with uncertainty,
but she was finally ready to contact
her birth mother. The discovery
brought about a mix of excitement
and trepidation, a strange
combination of anticipation and fear.

She wrote the letter with trembling
hands, her words tentative, hesitant,
filled with a mixture of hope and

apprehension. The letter was an attempt to reach across the vast chasm of years and secrets, a plea for connection, for understanding, for a piece of herself that had been missing for too long. She held her breath as she dropped the letter into the mailbox, her fate now sealed, her future intertwined with a woman she had only known as a phantom in the shadows of her memories. The wait that followed felt interminable, a suspended state where time stretched and her emotions ebbed and flowed, a maelstrom of hope and fear.

The letter arrived on a Tuesday, nestled amongst the usual bills and junk mail. Angela, perched on the worn porch swing of her modest cottage, barely registered its presence at first. The faded ink on the envelope was barely legible, the handwriting unfamiliar yet somehow... haunting. She almost tossed it aside, another unwanted intrusion into her carefully constructed solitude. But something stayed her hand, a flicker of unease, a prickle of recognition in the subtle curve of a particular letter, a familiar slant that echoed a forgotten past.

Hesitantly, she tore open the envelope, her heart thudding a frantic rhythm against her ribs. The paper inside, crisp and new, was a stark contrast to the weathered wood of the swing. The words, written in elegant cursive, were concise, yet brimming with a poignant vulnerability that resonated with a deep-seated tremor of her own long-buried pain. They spoke of a woman searching for her roots, a young woman named Jessica, a woman who possessed the same piercing hazel eyes Angela had long since tried to erase from her memory, eyes that mirrored her own, but held a depth of understanding that Angela herself had never reached.

The words detailed a shared birth date, a mention of an orphanage, a vague recollection of a town she'd never heard of a trail of crumbs leading back to her. Each detail chipped away at the carefully constructed wall of denial she had built around herself, slowly revealing the chasm of pain that had been festering beneath. The letter wasn't an accusation; it was a plea, a fragile olive branch extended across the vast expanse of time and unanswered questions. It was a lifeline thrown to a woman who had been adrift at sea for twenty-five years.

Angela reread the letter several times, the simple words taking on a different meaning with each pass.

The initial numbness gave way to a surge of panic, then a crushing wave of guilt. The weight of her past actions pressed down on her, heavy and suffocating, threatening to drown her in a sea of regret. The peaceful façade of her existence shattered, fragments of memories resurfacing like ghosts from a forgotten nightmare.

She saw herself, a young, terrified woman, her body bruised and spirit broken, cradling a newborn child whose innocent face mirrored her own terror and despair. The image was vivid, intensely real, a constant reminder of the irrevocable choice she had made, a choice that had shaped her life in ways she could never have anticipated. The weight of that decision, the pain of that abandonment, continued to plague her, threatening to consume her.

Days turned into weeks, the letter lying on her kitchen table, a silent, accusing presence. She couldn't bring herself to respond, paralyzed by fear and shame. The prospect of facing Jessica, of confronting the consequences of her actions, was unbearable. She was a master of avoidance, a woman who had built her life on lies and omissions, skilled at keeping her past buried beneath layers of silence and self-deception. The idea of facing Jessica, the young woman whose life she'd irrevocably altered, felt like stepping into a fiery pit.

But Jessica's persistence was unwavering. Another letter arrived, followed by a third, each one slightly more insistent, slightly more desperate. The final letter arrived accompanied by a phone number. It was a small gesture of connection but carried a palpable weight of hopefulness. She had no choice but to find a space for a conversation – even if it was with a stranger.

She chose a neutral ground: a small, unassuming coffee shop on the edge of town. It was a place she frequented, a haven of quiet anonymity, a place where she could blend into the background and remain unnoticed. But today, the familiar comfort was overshadowed by a rising tide of anxiety. She chose a secluded corner table, her hands trembling as she stirred her coffee, her heart hammering a frantic rhythm against her ribs. She felt a mixture of dread and anxiety. The coffee was cold, untouched, a reflection of her own internal state.

Jessica arrived precisely at the appointed time, her presence a shock of energy in the otherwise quiet café. She was everything Angela had imagined and more –

beautiful, intelligent, bearing an uncanny resemblance to her younger self, yet with a resilience, a maturity that Angela had never possessed. As Jessica approached, Angela felt the years melt away, a flood of memories and emotions threatening to overwhelm her. She barely managed a nod, her voice a strained whisper as she mumbled a greeting and put out her hand for a handshake. Hardly the type of first meeting Jessica had hoped to have.

Jessica, however, seemed unfazed by Angela's coolness. Her eyes, hazel like her mother's, held a quiet strength, a deep well of understanding that softened the blow of Angela's initial coldness. She smiled, a tentative, hopeful gesture that belied the apprehension in her own heart. "It's... it's good to finally meet you," she said, her voice calm and measured, defying the turmoil of emotions Angela felt within her.

Angela struggled to find a response, her throat constricting, her words failing her. She fumbled with her coffee cup, spilling some onto the table, a clumsy, desperate attempt to deflect the intense gaze that sought to pierce through her carefully constructed defenses. The silence stretched, an awkward, painful space filled only with the low hum of conversation from other patrons and the faint clinking of mugs. Angela knew it was going to be hard, but not this hard.

Jessica, sensing Angela's discomfort, spoke again, her voice soft but resolute. "I understand if you need time," she said gently. "I just wanted to meet you, to see what it felt like, finally. To know whether we share something. But I have no expectations, really. I wanted to give you the opportunity to explain your own perspective. My adoptive parents always told me that it's not worth holding onto grudges and that there are always two sides to every story. I hope you will tell me yours."

Angela looked at her, seeing not an accuser, but a woman who desperately wanted to understand. She saw a reflection of her own youthful vulnerability in the earnest expression on Jessica's face, a vulnerability she had long since buried beneath layers of hardened indifference. It was the most honest thing she had seen in a long time. She saw the hope and desperation in Jessica's eyes. The tears welling up in her own eyes were tears of regret, guilt and fear. She had spent so many years in self-imposed isolation, and this young woman, this kind stranger, was showing her a different path. Angela desperately wanted to connect with Jessica but her long standing guilt, shame and fear just wouldn't let her.

The weight of Jessica's silence pressed down on Angela, heavy and suffocating, but Jessica's words had carved a small crack in her emotional defenses. The small gesture of kindness had touched something within Angela. She felt a flicker of something she hadn't felt in a very long time: hope. The road ahead was undoubtedly arduous; there were many years of hurt and pain to confront, many lies to unravel, but with Jessica sitting across from her, she felt a flicker of something akin to compassion—a strange kind of hope for the future. The moment held a heavy weight of possibilities and the future was full of uncertainty. It was a long road ahead, but this first step had been taken.

The air hung heavy between them, thick with unspoken words and the ghosts of twenty-five years. Angela, her hands clasped tightly in her lap, felt the weight of those years pressing down on her, a physical burden she couldn't seem to shake. The coffee shop, once a sanctuary of quiet anonymity, now felt like a suffocating cage, the gentle hum of background noise amplifying the deafening silence between her and her daughter.

Jessica, however, remained composed, her gaze unwavering, a quiet strength emanating from her that both intimidated and strangely comforted Angela. She leaned forward, her voice barely a whisper, as if afraid to break the fragile equilibrium of the moment. "I understand if you don't want to talk about it," she said, her words carefully chosen, infused with a sensitivity that surprised Angela. "But I… I need to understand. I need to know why."

The question hung in the air, a simple yet profound inquiry that cut through Angela's carefully constructed defenses. She flinched, her eyes darting away from Jessica's intense gaze. The years of silence, the years of carefully built lies, felt like a suffocating weight pressing down on her chest. She opened her mouth to speak, but no words came. The memories, long suppressed, threatened to overwhelm her, a torrent of emotions threatening to break the dam she had built so meticulously around her heart.

"It wasn't... it wasn't easy," she finally managed, her voice a raspy whisper, barely audible above the gentle murmur of the coffee shop.

The words were inadequate, pathetically weak in the face of the monumental weight of her actions. She took a deep breath, trying to gather her composure, trying to find a way to articulate the pain, the terror, the despair that had driven her to make the most devastating decision of her life.

She began to speak, her voice trembling at first, then gaining strength as the words flowed, a torrent of confession pouring forth. She spoke of Johnathan, the man who had stolen her youth, her innocence, her very soul. She described the years of abuse, the physical and emotional violence that had left her scarred, broken, and utterly devoid of hope. She recounted the betrayal, the humiliation, the constant fear that had become her constant companion.

She spoke of the rape, the unwanted pregnancy, the sheer terror that had gripped her as she realized she was carrying another child of her abuser. She spoke of the desperation, the utter hopelessness that had consumed her, driving her to the edge of sanity. She described the feeling of utter isolation, devoid of any support or understanding. She had a network of family but was too ashamed to reach out.

"I was lost," she confessed, her voice cracking with emotion. "I didn't know what to do. I was young, terrified, and completely alone. I felt utterly abandoned and betrayed and that I could not protect my children."

Jessica listened intently, her expression a mixture of sympathy and understanding. She didn't interrupt, didn't offer platitudes or empty reassurances. She simply listened, her presence a silent testament to her empathy, her unwavering desire to understand the woman who had given her life. Her gaze, however, remained questioning. She had listened to her mother's story and there were some parts that made sense, other parts remained shrouded in mystery. She still felt a need to ask some difficult questions.

"But... abandoning me," Jessica finally said, her voice soft but firm. "Why? Why did you give me up?"

The question hung in the air, a sharp, piercing arrow that struck at the heart of Angela's guilt. She hesitated, her eyes welling up with tears. The memory of leaving Jessica, of falsely reporting her death, was a wound that had never healed, a raw, gaping chasm in her soul.

"I… I was afraid," she whispered, the words barely audible. "I was afraid for your safety, for your future. I thought… I thought it would be better for you to be with someone else, someone who could give you a better life than I could ever provide."

The explanation was weak, unconvincing even to her own ears. It was a flimsy justification for a horrific act, a desperate attempt to mitigate the immense guilt she carried within her. But it was the truth, as far as she could articulate it; a truth shrouded in the layers of trauma and self-deception she had lived with for so long.

Jessica listened, her expression unreadable. Then, she leaned forward, her voice hushed, conspiratorial. "Did anyone know?"

Angela's eyes widened slightly. The question hung heavy in the air between them. The unspoken truth was a heavy weight on Angela's soul. "No," she whispered. "No one ever knew, not even your father. It was my secret to carry."

Johnathan had passed away ten years prior to this meeting. That meant he died thinking Jessica died in that hospital. Anger and sadness came over Jessica knowing that her father never knew she was alive.

Jessica nodded slowly, absorbing her mother's words. A sense of understanding, of empathy washed over Angela. Jessica understood that the pain Angela was carrying was immense. The weight of that secret had to have been crushing.

"I want to understand," Jessica said softly. "I want to know everything." The conversation continued, a slow, painful excavation of buried memories, of unspoken truths and long-held secrets. Angela spoke of her own troubled childhood, of the emotional neglect and lack of support that had left her vulnerable to Johnathan's abuse. She spoke of the shame, the guilt, the overwhelming sense of failure that had consumed her after the birth of Jessica. The abandonment had been driven by a deep-seated fear that she would not be able to provide adequate care.

The conversation continued for hours. The coffee shop became a silent witness to a mother's confession, a daughter's quest for understanding, and a long-overdue confrontation between two souls long separated by pain and secrets. As the sun began to set, casting long shadows across the café, a sense of fragile understanding began to emerge from the depths of their shared pain. The road ahead remained long and arduous, but for the first time in twenty-five years, Angela felt a glimmer of hope, a faint possibility of healing, of forgiveness, of reconciliation. The path toward healing and forgiveness would not be easy, but together, mother and daughter began to walk. The pain of the past was still raw, but the possibility of a different future was a flickering ember in the darkness. The first step had been made, and though a long way lay ahead, they had both found a place to start. The weight of the secret, long carried by Angela alone, was beginning to shift, to be shared, to be understood. The chasm that separated them was vast, but for now, a bridge had been built.

The weight of Angela's confession settled heavily between them, a palpable silence replacing the gentle murmur of the coffee shop. Jessica, her face pale but composed, stared out the window, the bustling city street a blur outside the glass. The afternoon sun cast long shadows across the table, highlighting the stark contrast between the vibrant life outside and the emotional turmoil unfolding within the small, enclosed space. Angela watched her daughter, a mixture of hope and trepidation churning within her. This wasn't the reconciliation she had envisioned, the tearful embrace she'd perhaps fantasized about for years. This was raw, honest, and deeply painful.

Finally, Jessica turned, her gaze steady, unwavering. "The hospital… you said you had a miscarriage," she said, her voice barely a whisper, the words carrying the weight of years of unanswered questions, of a carefully constructed lie that had shattered her life. "But you didn't."

Angela flinched. The lie, once a shield, now felt like a shackle binding her to the past. "I… I couldn't face it," she admitted, her voice barely audible. "The shame, the guilt… it was too much. I couldn't bear the thought of everyone knowing."

"Everyone?" Jessica's voice was quiet, almost disbelieving. Angela shook her head, tears welling in her eyes. "No one knew," she whispered. "Not your father, not my family… no one. I carried that secret alone, for twenty-five years."

The enormity of that revelation hit Jessica like a physical blow. Twenty-five years of silence, twenty-five years of lies, twenty-five years of carrying a secret so profound that it had shaped her entire life. A wave of anger, a simmering resentment that she'd never acknowledged, rose within her. It wasn't just the abandonment; it was the deception, the systematic erasure of her existence, the fabrication of her death.

"But why?" she asked, her voice trembling with a mixture of hurt and outrage. "Why not tell anyone? Why fake my death?"

Angela hesitated, struggling to articulate the tangled web of emotions that had driven her actions. It wasn't simply fear; it was a complex cocktail of shame, guilt, and a deep-seated belief in her own inadequacy. Johnathan's abuse had eroded her self-worth, leaving her feeling unworthy of love, incapable of providing a safe and nurturing environment for her children. The pregnancy, a brutal reminder of his violence, had pushed her to the brink.

"I was broken, Jessica," she confessed, her voice breaking. "I felt like I didn't deserve you. I was terrified that you would suffer because of me, because of what happened. I thought it would be better for you to be with a loving family, to have a life free from the shadow of my past."

Jessica listened, her expression unreadable. She had to reconcile her own memories, a void where she should have had a childhood with her biological mother, filled instead with unanswered questions, with a sense of abandonment and a deep need to know who she was and where she belonged. She saw the fragility of her mother, a woman shattered by trauma. There was no easy answer to her anger. She felt the pain of her mother; the same pain her mother had passed down to her. The weight of her mother's past was now her own burden as well.

"But a life free from the shadow of your past meant a life where I didn't even exist," Jessica countered, her voice soft but firm. "You erased me. You denied me my history, my identity. And you did it without even telling anyone."

The words hung in the air, sharp and accusing. Angela winced, the truth of Jessica's statement cutting through her carefully constructed defenses. She had not only abandoned her daughter; she had also stolen her right to a past, to a family, to a sense of belonging. The weight of that realization was almost unbearable.

The conversation continued, a slow, painful excavation of buried memories, of unspoken truths and long-held secrets. Angela confessed the extent of Johnathan's cruelty, the constant fear that had haunted her life, the crushing isolation that had made her believe she had no other choice. She described her attempts to disappear, to erase herself from everyone's lives.

Jessica listened, offering no judgment, only a quiet empathy that was both unexpected and profoundly comforting. She had to understand. She had to accept the woman who had created her and abandoned her, at the same time. Her past was a puzzle with missing pieces, and this was just one piece. She would have to understand all of it. She began to understand how her mother's life shaped the choices she made. She needed to piece it all together. She needed more details; there were more questions.

As the sun dipped below the horizon, casting a warm glow across the city, a fragile understanding began to emerge from the ashes of their shared pain. It wasn't a reconciliation; it was a beginning. A tentative first step on a long and arduous journey toward healing. The weight of the secret, long carried alone by Angela, was slowly shifting. It was being shared, acknowledged, and tentatively, understood. The wounds remained, deep and raw, but a glimmer of hope pierced the darkness. The chasm between them was still vast, but at least, for the first time, they had begun to build a bridge. The journey towards healing, reconciliation, and forgiveness was long, full of emotional pitfalls and obstacles. However, in the quiet sharing, the mutual understanding, and the beginnings of acceptance, the possibility of healing became less of a far-fetched dream and more of a tenuous reality, within reach. The possibility of peace lay in their shared pain. The first step of a journey of a thousand miles had been taken. The journey would continue for a long time.

The silence that followed was heavy, thick with unspoken accusations and lingering regrets. Jessica reached for her coffee cup, her hand trembling slightly. The warmth of the ceramic felt strangely inadequate against the chill that had settled deep in her bones. She hadn't anticipated this – the raw, unvarnished truth spilling out from her mother, a torrent of confession that left her feeling both devastated and strangely… understood.

Angela watched her, her eyes brimming with unshed tears. The years of carefully constructed walls, the years of solitude and self-imposed exile, had crumbled in the face of Jessica's unwavering gaze. She had expected anger, outrage, perhaps even hatred. But Jessica's response, a quiet, almost contemplative sadness, surprised her. It was a sadness that mirrored her own, a shared grief for a life that had never been.

"I… I don't know what to say," Jessica finally whispered, her voice barely audible above the low hum of conversation in the coffee shop. The bustling city outside seemed a world away, a stark contrast to the intimate, emotionally charged space they occupied.

Angela reached across the table, her hand hovering hesitantly above Jessica's. The gesture was tentative, almost fearful, as if she anticipated rejection. Jessica met her gaze, a flicker of something akin to forgiveness in her eyes. She placed her hand over Angela's, a silent acknowledgment of their shared pain.

"I know," Angela murmured, her voice thick with emotion. "There's nothing you can say that will make it right. I understand if you can't forgive me."

The confession that followed was a slow, agonizing process, a peeling back of layers of deceit and self-deception. Angela described the escalating abuse she had suffered at the hands of Johnathan, the fear that had consumed her, the feeling of utter helplessness that had driven her to such desperate measures. She spoke of the isolation, the loneliness, the crushing weight of her secret, a burden she had carried alone for a quarter of a century. It wasn't simply a story of abandonment; it was a narrative of trauma, of a woman broken and desperate, clinging to the illusion that protecting her daughter meant erasing her entirely.

Jessica listened, absorbing the raw details of her mother's past. The anger she had felt earlier began to give way to a dawning understanding, a recognition of the immense pain that had driven Angela's actions. She learned of the constant fear, the emotional abuse, the physical violence. She saw not just the act of abandonment, but the broken woman who had perpetrated it, a woman who had been stripped of her own agency and self-worth.

"It wasn't just about me, was it?" Jessica said softly, her voice tinged with a newly acquired empathy. "It was about escaping... escaping all of it."

Angela nodded, tears streaming down her face. "Yes," she whispered. "I thought I was saving you from what I was living through."

"But you saved me into a void," Jessica replied. "You saved me into non-existence."

The statement hung in the air, a stark reminder of the profound impact of Angela's actions. There was no easy way to reconcile the pain of abandonment with the understanding of the circumstances that led to it. The conversation continued late into the evening, a painful, fragmented exploration of a life marked by abuse, betrayal, and loss. Angela revealed the details of her subsequent life – the years spent in isolation, the struggle to find solace, the crushing weight of guilt that had threatened to consume her. Jessica learned of her mother's attempts at rebuilding her life, her struggles with self-doubt, and her constant battle with the memories of her past.

As the sun began its descent, casting long shadows across the city, Jessica stood up. She was exhausted from the emotional turmoil, yet strangely invigorated, as if a heavy weight had been lifted. There was a lot to process. There were many more questions to ask, more details to uncover, more pieces of the puzzle to fall into place. This was only the beginning. The road ahead was uncertain and potentially arduous, but the path to understanding and perhaps even reconciliation had opened up.

Jessica's next step was a visit to the adoption agency that had placed her as a baby. She needed access to her adoption file, to see the records, the photographs of her as a baby. She needed more context, more details. She wanted to understand her mother's life completely, not only to understand her, but to understand herself in the context of her heritage, her family, her history.

The agency was sterile, cold and impersonal, a stark contrast to the emotional intensity of her conversation with her mother. The files were impersonal as well, filled with bureaucratic language and detached assessments. Yet amongst the factual records, she found hints, fragments of information that gave glimpses into the life she hadn't known. She saw the photographs of

her as a newborn, tiny and helpless,
a testament to the life she'd been
denied – the life she was finally
beginning to discover. The details of
her adoption, the circumstances of
her placement, and the profile of the
family who had adopted her were
all there. She found the letters
written by Angela, which spoke of
her regret and remorse, of her
desperate desire to protect her
daughter while not having the
strength to parent her. The
information felt raw and exposed, as
if someone had peeled back the
layers of Jessica's own life, a life
which was beginning to take shape.
The puzzle pieces started to come
together, revealing a more complete
picture of her past.

She also learned about the family
who adopted her; their lives, their
aspirations, their reasons for
wanting to adopt a child. The

records revealed a loving and nurturing environment that had given her the gift of a stable and caring upbringing. It was a testament to their strength and generosity that had allowed her to grow into the person she had become, filling the void left by her birth mother.

Leaving the agency, Jessica felt a profound sense of peace. She understood her mother's choices, not condoning them but comprehending them within the context of Angela's own suffering and trauma. She had also learned to appreciate the life she'd been given; a loving family, a supportive environment, and the opportunity to thrive.

She did not forgive Angela immediately, but understood her. The pain of abandonment remained, a deep scar on her soul, but she was also armed with a new understanding – an understanding that allowed her to move forward, to begin to heal from a past she'd never truly known, and to forge a future where her identity and her story were no longer hidden in the shadows of her mother's secrets, but were a story that she would write herself, from here on out. The journey would be long, but she was now more certain than ever of where she wanted to go. The path toward healing, although uncertain, had begun.

Chapter 3: Redemption or Isolation?

The salt spray stung Angela's face as she stood on the cliff overlooking the turbulent ocean. The wind, a relentless force, mirrored the turmoil within her. Twenty-five years. Twenty-five years she'd carried this secret, this crushing weight of guilt, this agonizing burden of abandonment. The ocean, vast and unforgiving, seemed a fitting metaphor for the depths of her remorse. She'd come to this spot, a place etched in her memory from her childhood, a place of both solace and terror, to finally confront the ghosts of her past.

The therapist's words echoed in her mind: "Facing your trauma is not about blame, Angela. It's about understanding. It's about reclaiming your narrative." But understanding felt so elusive. She understood the abuse, the fear, the desperation that had driven her to leave Jessica. But the act itself – the act of abandoning her own child – remained a monstrous, unforgivable act, a jagged tear in the fabric of her being.

She closed her eyes, the wind whipping her hair across her face. Images flooded her mind: Johnathan's leering face, the sickening violence, the pervasive fear that clung to her like a second skin. The memories were sharp, vivid, searing – a constant reminder of the life she'd barely escaped, a life that had stolen her youth, her spirit, her sense of self. She remembered the moment she placed Jessica in the bassinet at the adoption agency, the cold, sterile environment a chilling contrast to the warmth that should have filled her heart. The lie she had told – the fabricated story of Jessica's death – felt like a heavy stone in her chest, a constant reminder of her deception.

The PTSD had been a silent companion for years, a shadow lurking in the corners of her mind. Nightmares plagued her, vivid flashbacks of the abuse replaying themselves on the stage of her sleep. Anxiety gnawed at her, a constant state of hypervigilance, leaving her perpetually on edge, unable to fully relax. The fear of abandonment, ironically, had manifested itself in her own abandonment of her child, a cruel paradox that twisted the knife in her soul. She had learned to isolate, to build walls around herself, to protect herself from the pain of vulnerability, the pain of connection.

But Jessica's presence had shattered those walls. The conversation in the coffee shop, the raw honesty, the unexpected understanding – these had opened a crack in her carefully constructed fortress of solitude. Jessica's quiet sadness, her lack of vitriol, her willingness to understand—it was a revelation. It had given Angela a fragile hope, a flicker of possibility that maybe, just maybe, redemption wasn't entirely beyond reach.

The wind howled, a mournful symphony of the sea. Angela looked down at the crashing waves, the relentless rhythm of the ocean a mirror of her own internal struggle. She realized that healing wasn't a linear process; it wasn't a simple matter of erasing the past. It was a messy, chaotic, painful process of confronting the demons within, of accepting responsibility for her actions, of learning to forgive herself – a process she was only just beginning.

The seagulls cried overhead, their cries piercing the howling wind. She thought of Jessica, of the life she had been denied, of the years of silence and uncertainty that had marked Jessica's existence. The guilt was still immense, a leaden weight in her stomach. But mixed with the guilt, a new emotion was taking root: a desperate longing to mend the broken bonds, a desire to make amends, even if it meant facing the consequences of her actions.

She had spent years believing that silence was her only defense, that hiding the truth would protect Jessica, protect herself. Now, she understood that silence was a form of self-punishment, a form of isolation that only amplified her pain. The truth, however painful, was a necessary step toward healing, toward reconciliation, toward the possibility of redemption.

She thought of the adoption agency records, Jessica's quiet determination to understand her past. The records hadn't provided all the answers, but they provided a vital context, a missing piece in the jigsaw puzzle of Jessica's life, and perhaps, of her own. She had learned that the adoptive family had loved Jessica, provided her with a stable and loving home. This did not erase Angela's actions, but it provided a glimmer of hope – a confirmation that Jessica had thrived despite her abandonment.

Angela reached into her pocket, pulling out a worn, faded photograph. It was a picture of Jessica as a baby, a tiny, helpless infant with eyes that held a surprising wisdom. The image brought a fresh wave of guilt, a sharp pang of remorse, but also a profound sense of longing. She craved the opportunity to truly know Jessica, to understand the person she had become, to build a connection that had been cruelly denied for so many years.

She spent hours on the cliff, the wind whipping around her, the waves crashing at her feet. The ocean's vastness seemed to both intimidate and soothe her, reflecting the complexity of her emotions – guilt, remorse, fear, and a nascent hope. It was a journey of self-discovery, a painful reckoning with the consequences of her choices, a difficult and arduous task of rebuilding herself from the fragments of a shattered past.

The setting sun cast long shadows, painting the sky in hues of orange and purple. As darkness began to fall, Angela felt a shift within her. It wasn't a sudden, miraculous transformation; it was a subtle change, a quiet acknowledgement of the immense work that lay ahead. She wouldn't erase the past, but she could choose how to move forward. She could choose to confront her demons, to face her responsibilities, to strive for reconciliation, to seek forgiveness – not only from Jessica, but from herself.

The path to redemption would be long and arduous. It would require courage, humility, and a willingness to confront the deepest wounds of her past. But for the first time in a long time, Angela felt a glimmer of hope, a faint light piercing the darkness of her self-imposed exile. She wouldn't promise a happy ending, she wouldn't pretend that the pain would simply disappear. But she would face her truth. She would face her daughter. And she would begin the long, arduous, but necessary, journey towards healing and, perhaps, redemption. The ocean roared its approval, a symphony of both destruction and renewal. And Angela, facing into the growing darkness, knew that this was only the beginning. The journey towards her own reckoning had begun.

The therapist's soft voice cut through Jessica's swirling thoughts, a gentle anchor in the storm within. "Tell me about your anger, Jessica. It's okay to feel it."

Jessica hesitated, her gaze fixed on the worn, floral pattern of the therapist's carpet. Anger. It was a constant companion, a simmering resentment that threatened to boil over at any moment. Anger at Angela, the mother who had abandoned her, the mother whose existence was both a blessing and a curse. Anger at the cruel irony of a life shaped by a love that was never fully given. Anger at the years of uncertainty, the unanswered questions, the gnawing void where a mother's love should have been.

"It's… it's like a knot in my stomach," she finally whispered, her voice barely audible. "It tightens, then loosens, then tightens again. Sometimes it's a dull ache, sometimes it's a burning rage. I feel like I'm drowning in it."

Dr. Evans nodded sympathetically. "And what does that anger feel like physically? Where do you feel it in your body?"

Jessica closed her eyes, focusing on the sensations. "It's in my chest, mostly. Like a heavy weight, pressing down on my lungs. Sometimes it spreads to my shoulders, making them tense and stiff. It's exhausting."

Dr. Evans listened patiently, offering validating words and insightful questions, helping Jessica dissect the complex layers of her emotion. She explored the roots of Jessica's anger, gently guiding her towards understanding its origins in the trauma of abandonment. It wasn't just anger at Angela; it was a multifaceted emotion born from years of unanswered questions, a confusing mix of betrayal, confusion, and the persistent aching void left by a missing maternal figure. It was anger at the injustice of it all, the unfairness of being cast aside, of having her identity shaped by a secret she wasn't privy to.

The sessions weren't easy. There were days when Jessica felt overwhelmed by the intensity of her emotions, days when the tears flowed freely, days when she felt like giving up, questioning the point of it all. But Dr. Evans provided a safe space, a place where Jessica could express her pain without judgment, where she could begin to process the trauma that had shaped her life.

Slowly, gradually, Jessica began to understand. She began to see that her anger wasn't a sign of weakness; it was a natural response to the deep wound of abandonment. It was a powerful emotion, a testament to her resilience, a force that could propel her toward healing. And as she began to understand her anger, she began to understand herself.

Beyond the anger, there was grief. A deep, abiding grief for the mother she never knew, for the childhood she never had, for the connection that had been brutally severed. This grief manifested in unexpected ways. It wasn't the dramatic, tearful outpouring she had anticipated; instead, it was a quiet sadness, a subtle melancholy that permeated her days. It was a sense of loss, a feeling of incompleteness, a yearning for a connection that would likely never be fully realized.

Through guided imagery and journaling, Dr. Evans helped Jessica explore this grief, to acknowledge its presence without judgment, to allow herself to feel the sadness, the pain, the longing. It was a slow, painstaking process, a journey of emotional excavation. Jessica started keeping a journal, filling its pages with her thoughts, her feelings, her memories, both real and imagined. She described her ideal mother, her fantasies of having a loving family, contrasting them with the pain and emptiness she had been carrying for years. The journal became her confidante, a safe space to explore the landscape of her emotions.

She learned to differentiate between her anger and her grief, recognizing that they were two separate yet interwoven threads in the fabric of her emotional tapestry. It was a process of untangling, separating the strands of her trauma to examine each piece, to analyze and understand it. She learned to accept that the mother she longed for was an idealized image, a construct based on her hopes and wishes, not a reflection of Angela's reality.

In the support group, Jessica found a community of women who had also experienced the trauma of abandonment. Hearing their stories, sharing their experiences, and recognizing that she wasn't alone in her pain, proved incredibly healing. It was a powerful reminder that the pain she felt wasn't unique; it was a shared experience, a common thread uniting them in their journey of healing. The support group wasn't just about sharing pain; it was about creating a space of understanding, mutual support, and healing. It was a space where Jessica felt safe, accepted, and understood. She wasn't alone in her struggle.

The women shared their stories of overcoming adversity, of finding strength and resilience in the face of unimaginable challenges. Jessica listened, absorbing their wisdom, drawing strength from their experiences. She began to see that healing wasn't about erasing the past; it was about accepting it, learning from it, and moving forward.

As the weeks turned into months, a gradual shift began to take place within Jessica. The anger began to subside, replaced by a quiet determination. The grief, while still present, became less overwhelming, less consuming. She started to focus on self-care, on nurturing her own well-being. She took up yoga, rediscovering the quiet strength of her body. She began to paint, expressing her emotions through vibrant colors and bold strokes. She cultivated friendships, building meaningful connections with people who valued and supported her.

One evening, as she sat on her balcony, gazing at the sunset, a profound sense of peace settled over her. The knot in her stomach had loosened, the weight on her chest had lifted. She realized that she hadn't forgotten the pain, but she had learned to live with it, to integrate it into her life, to view it not as a defining characteristic, but as a catalyst for growth. She was still on a journey, but she felt a renewed sense of hope, a sense of self-acceptance.

Jessica had found her strength not in denying her past but in confronting it, understanding it, and ultimately, accepting herself despite it. Her journey wasn't a straight path; it had been winding and difficult, filled with emotions that threatened to overwhelm her. Yet, through therapy, support groups, and self-reflection, she learned to navigate her feelings, to find acceptance, and to discover a new, empowered version of herself. She understood now that healing was a continuous process, but she was ready to embrace it, a strong, determined woman prepared to step into her future. She wouldn't forget what happened, but she would not be defined by it. She was ready to meet Angela on her terms.

The meeting took place in a small, sun-drenched café overlooking a tranquil park. It wasn't the grand, emotionally charged confrontation Jessica had imagined. Instead, it felt strangely ordinary, almost mundane. The clinking of china, the murmur of conversations, the gentle rustling of leaves outside—all served as a muted backdrop to the seismic shift occurring between them.

Angela arrived first, her hands clasped tightly in her lap, her posture rigid, betraying the nervousness beneath her composed exterior. She was a woman etched by time, her face a roadmap of hardship and regret. Jessica, watching from a nearby table, felt a pang of sympathy, a fleeting moment of understanding that transcended the anger and resentment that had long dominated her perspective. This wasn't the monstrous figure of her imagination, but a fragile woman, burdened by her own demons.

When Jessica approached, Angela didn't flinch, didn't look away. Her gaze, though hesitant, held a flicker of something akin to recognition, a fragile tendril of connection reaching across the chasm of years and unspoken words. The silence between them was thick, heavy with the weight of unspoken accusations and unfulfilled hopes. It wasn't a hostile silence, but one pregnant with unspoken emotions, a silence that spoke volumes of their shared history.

"Jessica," Angela began, her voice barely above a whisper, a tremor betraying her inner turmoil. The name, uttered after so many years, felt foreign yet familiar, a bridge between two fractured lives. "I… I didn't know how to contact you. I didn't know how to reach out."

Jessica met her gaze, her own emotions a tangled mess of anger, grief, and a surprising surge of compassion. "I found you," she replied, her voice steady, despite the trembling in her hands. "I wanted to understand." The words were simple, yet they carried the weight of a lifetime's longing.

The conversation was halting at first, punctuated by long silences, by nervous sips of coffee, by averted gazes. Angela spoke of her abusive marriage, of the desperation that had led to her actions. She spoke of the crushing weight of guilt, of the constant fear of discovery, of the self-imposed isolation that had become her prison. She didn't offer excuses, didn't attempt to justify her actions. She simply laid bare her pain, her vulnerability, allowing Jessica to witness the depth of her sorrow.

Jessica listened, her anger slowly dissolving into a profound sadness. She heard the echoes of her own pain in Angela's words, the shared experience of trauma, of loss, of the devastating impact of a broken family. She saw the broken woman, not the heartless mother of her imagination.

The hours that followed were a testament to the power of vulnerability and honesty. Jessica shared her own experiences, the years of uncertainty, the aching void left by Angela's absence. She described the anger, the grief, the relentless yearning for a connection that had been so cruelly denied. She spoke of the therapy, the support group, the arduous journey of healing. There were tears, of course, but they weren't tears of rage or resentment, but tears of shared pain, of understanding, of finally letting go.

The afternoon sun cast long shadows across the café as they talked, the conversation flowing more freely now, the chasm between them slowly narrowing. Angela revealed the details of Jessica's birth, of the agonizing decision she'd made, the crushing weight of her lie.

She spoke of the unbearable pain of giving her up, the guilt that had haunted her every waking moment. She spoke of her belief that she was protecting Jessica, shielding her from a life of instability and hardship.

Jessica's response wasn't immediate. There was a moment of intense silence, a moment of profound contemplation. This was the narrative she hadn't known, the other side of the coin. It was far from a justification, but it was an explanation. An explanation that, while not exonerating Angela, provided a framework for her understanding. It humanized Angela. It didn't excuse her actions, but it contextualized them.

"I never knew," Jessica whispered, her voice thick with emotion. "I never understood. I built a whole life based on what I imagined."

This acknowledgment was a turning point. It wasn't a simple declaration of forgiveness, but a recognition of Angela's humanity, a willingness to understand her perspective, even if it didn't fully excuse her actions. It was a letting go of the bitter resentment that had poisoned her life for so long.

The remainder of their time together was spent in a quiet contemplation of shared pain. There was no sudden burst of reconciliation, no dramatic resolution. The healing process was a slow, tender unfolding. They exchanged photographs, shared fragments of their lives, allowing each other to see the women they had become. Angela shared stories of her life after Johnathan, her slow rebuilding, the new path she had created for herself.

Jessica, in turn, spoke of her own life, her accomplishments, her dreams, the strength she had found in the face of adversity. They spoke of the future, of the tentative steps towards building a relationship, a relationship built not on denial, but on understanding, acceptance, and, gradually, the hope of forgiveness.

As they spoke, more questions started to fill Jessica's mind. Jessica had been so consume with trying to understand her mother until she totally forgot to ask about any siblings or what did Jonathan do after he left her and moved on. Jessica felt that maybe those questions were better saved for another meeting.

As they parted, there was no grand declaration, no dramatic scene. There was only a simple embrace, a fragile connection forged in the crucible of pain, a shared understanding that the road to forgiveness was a long and arduous one. But in that embrace, in the shared tear that fell down Angela's cheek, there was the faint, fragile promise of a future together, a testament to the enduring power of family ties, the possibility of healing, and the slow, painstaking process of finding redemption.

The sun had set, painting the sky in hues of orange and purple as Jessica walked away. The weight she carried felt lighter, the anger a distant echo. She knew this was just the beginning of a long journey, that the wounds of the past would not disappear overnight. But she carried with her a newfound sense of peace, a sense of hope for the future, a glimmer of possibility that where there had once been only pain and isolation, there might now be a path to healing, reconciliation, and the fragile, tentative beginnings of a family. The path was long and arduous, full of potential pitfalls and setbacks. Yet, as Jessica walked under the twilight sky, she felt a lightness in her step, an optimism that had been absent for far too long. The journey towards forgiveness had begun. It was a journey that would test her strength, her resilience, and her capacity for empathy. But she was ready. She had learned to embrace her strength, and to use it to build a future free from the shackles of the past. The meeting at the café was merely a steppingstone on a long path ahead. A path of understanding, acceptance, and perhaps, in time, forgiveness.

The following weeks were a blur of tentative steps and hesitant gestures. Angela, emboldened by their initial meeting, began to reach out more frequently. It wasn't easy. Each phone call was a small act of courage, each email a leap of faith. The fear of rejection, of Jessica withdrawing, still lingered, a shadow at the edges of her newfound hope. But the desire to connect, to bridge the chasm that had separated them for so long proved stronger than her fear.

Their conversations became longer, more intimate. Angela shared details of her life after Johnathan – the grueling process of rebuilding her life, the slow, painful healing from the emotional wounds of her abusive marriage. She spoke of the work she did now as a counselor, helping other women escape abusive relationships, finding solace and purpose in helping others navigate the same treacherous waters she had once struggled to escape. She described the quiet satisfaction she found in her work, a quiet sense of redemption amidst the wreckage of her past. It was a testament to her resilience, a testament to her capacity for growth and healing.

Jessica, in turn, shared more about her life, her achievements, her dreams. She spoke of her work as a social worker, helping children and families navigate the complexities of foster care and adoption. She spoke of her own journey of healing, of therapy, of learning to trust, of building healthy relationships. The parallels between their lives – their shared experiences of trauma, loss, and the long road to healing – emerged not as points of contention, but as threads of connection, weaving a delicate tapestry of shared understanding.

Their conversations were often punctuated by long pauses, by silences that were not uncomfortable, but filled with a shared understanding of the unspoken pain that still lingered between them. There were tears, yes, but they were tears of shared vulnerability, tears that spoke of shared experiences and mutual healing, tears that eased the pain of years of separation. These were tears that brought them closer.

One Saturday afternoon, Angela invited Jessica to her small cottage, nestled in a quiet seaside village. The cottage, modest yet charming, was filled with sunlight and the scent of sea air. The garden, bursting with vibrant flowers, reflected a quiet beauty, a metaphor for the fragile new life Angela had carefully cultivated. Jessica had envisioned a grand, imposing house, reflecting

perhaps a wealth she assumed
Angela had gained from escaping
her abuse. The modest cottage,
however, was comforting in its
simplicity. It spoke of a quiet peace,
a sense of contentment.

As they sat in the garden, sipping
tea, Angela shared stories of her
childhood, stories that Jessica hadn't
known. They were stories of loss
and hardship, stories of a difficult
upbringing, and a childhood marred
by neglect and emotional distance. It
wasn't an attempt to excuse her
actions, but an explanation, a
context, an insight into the woman
who had made the impossible
decision to give her daughter up for
adoption. These stories brought
them closer; these were the stories
that showed Jessica the woman
behind the devastating actions, the
human being who had survived
against great odds.

That afternoon, they also spoke about Johnathan. The topic was difficult, the emotions still raw, but their conversation was surprisingly calm, free from the bitterness and anger that had once defined their relationship. Angela spoke openly about his cruelty, his infidelity, and the toxic nature of their marriage. She spoke of his manipulation and control, how it had slowly eroded her sense of self-worth. It was not only Angela's story, but a testament to the cyclical nature of abuse and the complexities of escape.

For Jessica, hearing Angela's story was a revelation. She saw her mother not just as a victim, but as a survivor, a woman who had endured unimaginable pain and emerged stronger, more resilient. The anger she had carried for so many years began to dissipate, replaced by a profound empathy

and compassion. She felt the
strength and resilience of the
woman who gave her up, a
resilience that echoed in her own
life.

Over the next few months, their
relationship deepened. They started
small, sharing photographs, texts,
and occasional phone calls.
Gradually, they began to share more
of their lives, their hopes, and their
dreams. They would talk for hours,
sharing stories of their work, their
friends, their passions. They would
delve into their favorite books, and
reminisce about the shared
memories that did exist. They had
discovered that they both had a
deep love for literature, an
unexpected connection that further
deepened their bond.

The most significant shift was in their perception of each other. Jessica began to see Angela not as the heartless mother who had abandoned her, but as a flawed, vulnerable woman who had made a terrible mistake driven by fear, desperation, and a deep-seated belief that she was protecting her daughter. Angela, in turn, saw Jessica not as the angry, resentful young woman she had anticipated, but as a strong, compassionate individual who had overcome her own trauma and emerged stronger and wiser.

One evening, as they talked on the phone, Jessica asked the question that had been lurking in her mind for months: "Why didn't you keep me? You kept my siblings"

The question was simple, yet it carried the weight of a lifetime of unspoken pain and longing. Angela's voice trembled as she answered, her words filled with raw emotion and deep regret. She spoke of the unrelenting abuse, the fear for her own safety, the crushing weight of poverty and desperation, and the overwhelming sense of hopelessness that had led her to make that devastating choice. She confessed that she had believed it was the only way to ensure Jessica's survival and well-being, shielding her from the turmoil of her own broken life. It wasn't a justification, but it was an explanation, born of raw honesty and deep remorse.

Jessica listened, her anger slowly dissolving into a profound sadness. She understood; or, at least, she was beginning to understand. She saw the agonizing choice her mother had made, the heart-wrenching decision that had been driven by fear and desperation. She heard the grief in her mother's voice.

Their conversations became less about accusations and more about understanding, acceptance, and the slow, painful process of forgiveness. It wasn't easy. There were moments of doubt, of hesitation, of lingering pain. But the foundation of their relationship was built on honesty, vulnerability, and a shared commitment to healing. They had built a bond founded on the resilience and strength of both women.

One summer evening, Jessica visited Angela's cottage again. As they sat by the seaside, watching the waves crash against the shore, Jessica placed her hand on her mother's. It wasn't a grand gesture of forgiveness, but a quiet acknowledgment of their shared journey, a recognition of the pain they had both endured, and the tentative beginnings of a new relationship. It was a connection forged in the crucible of pain, a quiet affirmation that the long, arduous journey toward healing and reconciliation had begun. The sun set, painting the sky with breathtaking colors, as mother and daughter sat in comfortable silence, finally at peace. This new beginning was tentative, fragile, and yet, undeniably hopeful.

As they sat there Jessica finally got up the courage to ask Angela, "have you told my siblings about me?" After a brief silence Angela finally answered no. Why, snapped Jessica! In a soft tone Angela stated that her brothers were in the military and she felt this was something they should hear in person. Both were expected to be home for a visit in a few months and that is when Angela planned on telling them.

Oddly enough this seemed to make sense to Jessica. This is a lot to take in and her brothers were both innocent in this. Angela told Jessica that when they came home she wanted her to be there when she told them. They deserve to know the truth. This gave Jessica a feeling of acceptance knowing that her mother wasn't trying to hide her existence again.

Over the next few years Jessica got to meet her siblings and eventually formed a bond with them. Angela was unsure of how the boys would take the news of what she did to Jessica, but much to her surprise they were understanding and accepting.

Five years later, the coastal cottage, once a symbol of Angela's quiet solitude, now bustled with a different kind of energy. Laughter, light, and the scent of baking bread replaced the previous quietude. Jessica, her face radiant with a happiness that mirrored Angela's own, helped her mother arrange flowers for a small family gathering. The garden, once a sanctuary for Angela's solitary reflection, now thrived under their shared care, a vibrant testament to their evolving bond.

This wasn't a fairytale ending, a sudden erasure of the past's harsh strokes. The scars remained, etched subtly on their faces, whispering tales of hardship and pain. The silence that sometimes settled between them wasn't awkward; it held the weight of shared experiences, the unspoken understanding that comes only with profound loss and hard-won healing. But within that silence, a new understanding had blossomed, a quiet acceptance that transcended the initial wounds.

Jessica's adopted family was part of this new life, an extended family that embraced Angela with warmth and respect. They understood the complexities of their relationship, the intricate tapestry woven from years of separation and the painstaking efforts to rebuild trust. There were still moments when the ghosts of the past crept into their present, whispers of Johnathan's abuse, fleeting reminders of the abandonment. But these moments were fleeting, overshadowed by the strength of their newly forged bond.

Angela, in her work as a counselor, found a deeper purpose, her experiences adding a layer of empathy and understanding that resonated deeply with her clients. She shared fragments of her journey, not to solicit pity, but to offer hope, to demonstrate that healing was possible, that even the most devastating experiences could be transmuted into strength and resilience. She found solace in empowering others to navigate the treacherous waters she had once traversed alone.

Jessica, too, had found her footing. Her work as a social worker was fulfilling, her compassion sharpened by her personal journey. She used her experiences to understand and support vulnerable children and families, bridging the gaps between broken systems and shattered hopes. She had learned to see the complexities of human behavior, the multifaceted reasons behind seemingly cruel actions. She understood that there was no easy formula for forgiveness, but that healing was a journey, not a destination.

One evening, as they sat on the porch overlooking the sea, Jessica mentioned Liam, a kind, gentle man who had become a significant part of her life. She spoke of their shared values, their mutual respect, and the quiet joy their relationship brought. Angela listened with quiet pride, a warmth spreading through her heart. She saw in Liam's presence a continuation of the resilience and strength that had always characterized her daughter. She was proud, not only of Jessica's accomplishments, but also of the person she had become, a testament to her inner strength.

The past, however, never truly disappeared. It lingered, a subtle undercurrent in their conversations, a faint echo in their shared silences. There were days when the weight of Angela's decision pressed heavily on her, the regret a tangible presence. Jessica, too, experienced moments of doubt, the lingering question of "why?" sometimes surfacing in the quiet moments, a reminder of the chasm that had once separated them. But their shared journey, their mutual commitment to understanding and healing, had forged a bond strong enough to weather the storms of their past.

It had been more than fifteen years since the passing of Jessica's biological father, Jonathan. After Jonathan left Angela, no one bothered to contact him or keep track of him. Angela knew he had moved to California but that was about all that she knew. Jessica remembered that Jonathan had a child with the woman he left Angela for, but little else was known. DNA testing had started to become popular now and could possibly answer some of the questions that Jessica had, but this meant opening another door into the unknown.

One day while sitting at her desk at work, Jessica decided to order a DNA test kit online. Now that Jessica had established a relationship with her mother's side of the family she figured it was time to find out about her father's side. Jessica knew she had to handle this delicately because as far as she knew her father's family either didn't know about her or they thought she had died at birth. Jessica didn't know if she would be accepted or rejected but she was prepared for either scenario.

After a few weeks, Jessica got an email from the DNA testing company informing her of some hits. After going to the companies website Jessica logged in for her results.

When Jessica logged in she couldn't believe her eyes. There he was, her top match, Darwin, her brother on her father's side. Jessica was both excited, yet nervous. Her first response was to immediately contact him but she held off. What if he didn't want to acknowledge her as his sibling? This new set of emotions was churning in Jessica's stomach like an upset stomach after a night of Mexican food. After carefully thinking it out Jessica decided to send the message and hope for the best.

As Jessica patiently waited for his response, she started to wonder who else was she going to find through

this DNA test. Are there more
siblings, grandparents, aunts,
uncles?

After two days Darwin finally
responded. His response was warm
and genuine. He said he knew his
father had other children but he
didn't know how to contact them.
He stated that after our father
passed he found an unmailed letter
in his personal items addressed to
Angela from him. Darwin stated
that he always wanted to give the
letter to Angela but he didn't know
where to send it. Darwin also
surprised me with some more news.
Our father had five children in
California after leaving Angela.

Jessica now had to have a seat. Five
more siblings? Wow! Jessica gave
Darwin Angela's address to forward
the letter and told Darwin she
needed a little time to let this all
digest. After ending her

conversation with Darwin, Jessica contacted Angela to tell her the news.

After a few days a letter arrived at Angela's home bearing a familiar name. It was from Darwin. Inside the envelope was the unmailed letter that Jonathan had addressed to Angela.

As Angela opened the envelope and started reading the letter, Jonathan's words were filled with remorse and regret, a belated attempt to mend a relationship that had long since crumbled beyond repair. Angela read the letter with a mixture of sadness and a profound sense of detachment. The anger she once felt was now muted, replaced by a weary understanding. She saw not a repentant man, but a shadow of the abusive past she had worked so tirelessly to escape. She didn't respond. The letter became a relic, a reminder of the life she had left behind, a life she no longer wished to revisit.

Jessica had seen the letter, too. She offered a comforting hand, a silent acknowledgment of the pain that lingered even within the quiet solace of their new-found peace. Their relationship had become a testament to their resilience, their shared history a constant reminder of their growth and healing. They had learned to coexist with the past, acknowledging its lingering presence without allowing it to define their present or future.

The cottage, though small, held the echo of their shared journey, the scent of forgiveness hanging in the air like a gentle mist. It was not just a physical dwelling, but a haven that had witnessed the slow, painstaking reconstruction of their lives and the delicate unfolding of their bond. It stood as a testament to the remarkable capacity for human resilience, a symbol of the enduring power of family ties, and a reminder that healing, even in the face of devastating loss, was always possible. Their story was not one of perfect resolution, but one of progress, a testament to the ongoing journey toward wholeness and acceptance, a future filled with the quiet understanding and enduring strength they had forged in the crucible of pain.

Jessica knew she had her work cut out for her. Locating the rest of her siblings and trying to put some closure to her story, but she was far from the end. The DNA test was merely the key which unlocked her family history.

Although Jonathan had long passed, Jessica still felt she needed closure. One day out of the blue Jessica booked a flight to California to visit Darwin and Jonathan's resting place in the military cemetery. Although his body had long left this earth, Jessica still felt his presence at his gravesite. The trip was short but filled with emotions. Jessica and Darwin made a promise to each other to locate the rest of their siblings and the family they never knew.

On the flight back, Jessica now had a renewed sense of purpose. To find was taken from her at birth. To make her life whole.

Years later, Angela and Jessica found themselves back at the seaside, not in the intimate setting of the cottage, but amidst the bustle of a family gathering. Jessica's children, bright-eyed and full of life, ran along the beach, their laughter carrying on the sea breeze. Angela watched them, a quiet smile playing

on her lips. She saw in their carefree
joy a reflection of the peace she had
finally found. She observed Jessica
interacting with her children, her
role as a mother both instinctive and
deeply fulfilling. Angela felt a sense
of completeness, an acceptance that
went beyond the initial pain of
separation.

The past was still there, a subtle
hum beneath the surface of their
lives, a reminder of the fragility of
happiness and the power of
resilience. But it no longer held the
power to define them, to control
their actions, or to dictate their
future. The echoes of the past were
faint, overshadowed by the strength
of their present and the hope for
their future. The journey towards
forgiveness had been long and
arduous, riddled with moments of
doubt and heartache. However, the
enduring strength of their bond,

their shared resilience, and their mutual commitment to healing had allowed them to build a relationship far stronger than the pain that had once separated them.

The sun set, casting long shadows across the beach, painting the sky in shades of orange and purple. Angela and Jessica stood side-by-side, their hands brushing against each other, a quiet acknowledgment of their shared journey, a silent testament to their enduring love. The waves crashed against the shore, their rhythmic roar a constant reminder of the enduring power of time and the inexorable passage of life. As they watched the sun sink below the horizon, they felt a sense of profound peace, a quiet acceptance that embraced both their past and their future, a future that was bright, albeit still marked by the delicate scars of their shared history. The ocean stretched before them, vast and limitless, a symbol of their own boundless capacity for growth and healing. Their story was a testament to the enduring power of the human spirit and the strength of family bonds, forged not in flawless perfection but through the crucible of pain, forgiveness, and the quiet acceptance of what life had brought. The future was uncertain, but it held a promise, an echo of hope whispered on the gentle sea breeze, a hope that grew stronger with each passing day.

As Jessica sat back, writing in her journal, she envisioned the day when she and all her siblings would get together for one big reunion.

Chapter Four: The Beginning of the End

Jessica and Darwin's journey to find their long-lost siblings was filled with both excitement and apprehension. Darwin had been separated from their family at a young age and, over time, had lost touch with all but a faint hope of reconnecting. But now with Jessica that hope had ignited into a burning desire to rebuild their family bonds.

Darwin, the older brother, had always felt a sense of responsibility for his younger siblings. He knew of their existence but had given up on ever finding them, believing that they had moved on with their lives and forgotten about him. Yet, seeing Jessica again made him realize that family ties could never truly be broken. Together, they set out on a path of discovery, determined to overcome the obstacles that had kept them apart for so long.

As they began their search, they encountered challenges and dead ends. Their inquiries seemed to lead nowhere, and they questioned whether their quest was futile. But their resilience and mutual support kept them going. They followed faint traces, vague memories, and whispered rumors, determined to leave no stone unturned in their quest for reunion.

As the days turned into weeks, Jessica and Darwin's determination only grew stronger. They navigated through a maze of old records and fading memories, their inquiries taking them to distant towns and forgotten corners of the country. Every new lead brought a mix of anticipation and uncertainty. They met people who offered snippets of information, some helpful, others leading them down false trails. Yet, they persevered, their bond strengthening with each challenge they faced.

One day, a chance encounter with an elderly woman in a remote village offered a glimmer of hope. She recalled a family that matched their description and directed them to an old farmhouse on the outskirts of town. As they approached the dilapidated building, a sense of Deja vu washed over Darwin. He remembered playing in the fields as a child, and a long-forgotten sense of belonging took root in his heart.

Inside the farmhouse, they met a woman named Maria, whose kind eyes and gentle spirit immediately put them at ease. She shared stories of her own family and expressed her regret at losing touch with her nieces and nephews. With each word, Jessica and Darwin felt a piece of the puzzle fall into place. They knew they had finally found their long-lost aunt, their father's sister, and with this discovery, they were one step closer to reuniting their family.

Jessica and Darwin exchanged eager glances as they stepped across the threshold of the old farmhouse, their hearts pounding with anticipation. The musty scent of aged wood and the soft creak of floorboards beneath their feet added to the sense of stepping back in time. Maria's gentle voice broke the silence, offering a warm welcome and inviting them to sit at the aged wooden table, its surface scarred by the passage of time. As they listened to Maria's stories, a thousand questions raced through their minds, each one carefully considered before being voiced.

With each answer, a new piece of their family history was revealed, like a tapestry being woven thread by thread. They learned of their parents' early struggles, the circumstances that had led to Jonathan's separation from their mothers, and the challenges Maria had faced in maintaining contact over the years. It was a story of love, loss, and resilience, and it filled in the gaps of their own life stories.

As the sun began to set, casting a golden glow over the farmhouse, Jessica and Darwin realized that they had found not only their long-lost aunt but also a treasure trove of family history and a deeper understanding of their own identities. The sense of belonging that Darwin had felt as a child playing in those fields was now a tangible reality. Their journey had not been in vain, and the obstacles they had overcome had only strengthened their resolve. Together, they would continue to rebuild their family bonds and ensure that their newly forged connections endured.

The sun had set, and the golden glow of dusk enveloped the farmhouse, marking the end of a momentous day. As Jessica and Darwin bid farewell to their aunt, Maria, their hearts were filled with a mélange of emotions. The warmth of familial love, the excitement of newfound connections, and the satisfaction of piecing together their family history—all coalesced within them. They had uncovered not just their long-lost aunt but also a repository of memories and a link to their past.

As they ventured back into the world, their journey was far from over. With Maria's help, they now had a trove of new leads and potential connections to explore. Each step brought them closer to completing the puzzle of their family tree and reuniting with their scattered siblings. The obstacles they had overcome and the resilience they had fostered fueled their determination to find the missing pieces of their family.

The brother-sister duo's quest had taught them that family bonds could transcend time and distance. With their aunt's guidance and their unwavering perseverance, they were ready to face the challenges that lay ahead. Their path was uncertain, but their resolve was steadfast. Together, they would navigate the twists and turns of their journey, knowing that their efforts would lead them to the heart of their family.

The journey ahead promised to be arduous, but Jessica and Darwin were prepared to face whatever challenges lay in store. Their newfound connection with Aunt Maria had fortified their resolve. As they bid her farewell, she bestowed upon them a trove of cherished mementos and letters, each one a tangible link to their family's past. Among them was an aged photograph, its edges frayed, depicting a young man who bore a striking resemblance to Darwin. It was their father, Jonathan, in his youth, and the resemblance between father and son was undeniable.

As they ventured forth, guided by Maria's wisdom and their own unwavering determination, they felt a sense of purpose and belonging that had eluded them for so long. Each step brought them closer to unraveling the mysteries of their family's history and reconnecting with their scattered siblings. The photograph of their father became a beacon, a reminder of the enduring nature of family bonds, and a symbol of the love that transcended time and distance.

The days turned into weeks and then months as Jessica and Darwin pursued every lead, their journey taking them across the country and into the hearts of those they encountered. Their story, one of resilience and hope, inspired others to reflect on the power of family and the enduring nature of love. Together, they navigated the twists and turns of their quest, their bond strengthening with each challenge overcome.
The challenges faced in locating Keisha and Amber. Detailing the various leads and dead ends encountered. Days turned into weeks and weeks into months but still no sign of Keisha and Amber.

The search for Keisha and Amber
had become increasingly difficult as
time marched on. Jessica and
Darwin refused to give up hope,
even as leads dried up. They
retraced their steps, revisiting places
that held memories, hoping for a
glimpse or a clue. They scoured the
city, following every tip, no matter
how unlikely. But each lead seemed
to evaporate, leaving them with
more questions than answers. The
sisters had seemingly vanished into
thin air, and the pain of their
absence grew heavier with each
passing day.

Months blended into seasons, and
the search took on a new urgency.
They refused to accept that their
sisters could be gone for so long
without a trace. They sought help
from professionals, investigators,
and even psychics, desperate for any
advantage. The investigation took
them down dark paths, revealing
secrets they wished had stayed
buried. Yet, despite their efforts, the
trail remained cold, and the sisters'

whereabouts remained a frustrating mystery.

As the search intensified, so did the realization of just how little they knew about their sisters. Keisha and Amber had lived their lives with a level of secrecy that seemed impossible to penetrate. The family was forced to confront the fact that their sisters may have chosen to disappear, but this thought only fueled their determination to find them. They continued their relentless quest, driven by love and worry, hoping that the next lead would be the one to bring their sisters home.

Jessica and Darwin's relentless search for their sisters, Keisha and Amber, had become a labyrinth of uncertainty and fading hopes. As they delved deeper into the mystery, they encountered a web of secrets and dead ends that seemed to taunt their every move. The siblings refused to yield, even as the trail grew colder with each passing

season. They navigated through a
maze of false leads and elusive
clues, their determination
unwavering.

The absence of Keisha and Amber
left a gaping hole in their family,
and the pain of their disappearance
weighed heavily on Jessica and
Darwin's hearts. They sought solace
in their shared purpose, comforting
each other in moments of doubt and
despair. Together, they retraced
their sisters' footsteps, poring over
every detail of their lives, no matter
how insignificant it seemed. But the
sisters had left few traces, and the
trail remained frustratingly obscure.

As the search intensified, Jessica and
Darwin discovered a hidden depth
to their sisters' lives that they had
never suspected. Keisha and Amber
had moved in mysterious circles,
their actions shrouded in secrecy.
The more they uncovered, the more
they realized how little they knew of
their sisters' true natures. It was as if
they were strangers hiding in plain

sight. Despite the mounting challenges, Jessica and Darwin remained steadfast in their quest, driven by an unyielding love and an unshakeable bond that kept their hope burning. Although their journey was not complete, Jessica and Darwin continued their search for their lost family.

Chapter Five: Tragedy

One day Jessica's phone rang, and it was Darwin with news about Keisha and Amber. It wasn't the news they were hoping to find but they did locate them. Keisha and Amber were both deceased.

Jessica's heart sank as she absorbed the news. She had been preparing herself for any outcome, but the finality of her sisters' deaths hit her hard. "How did it happen?" she asked, her voice steady despite the turmoil within. Darwin's voice was grim as he replied, "Apparently, they were involved in a car accident a few years ago. Keisha and Amber were both homeless and living in a car. One night while driving down the California coast their car went off the road and over a cliff. Since both of their mothers had lost contact with the family, no one on our father's side of the family knew.

Darwin continued, his voice softening as he sensed Jessica's distress. "I'm sorry, Jess. I know how much you wanted to meet them. We'll get through this together, just like we always do." Jessica nodded, grateful for her brother's unwavering support. Despite the pain, she felt a sense of relief that at least now they knew. The uncertainty and endless searching had been agonizing. Now, they could begin to process their grief and find a way to honor their sisters' memories.

As the initial shock wore off, Jessica's determination kicked in. "We need to contact the other siblings and let them know. It was a somber task, but one that brought the remaining siblings closer together. In their grief, they found solace in each other, and their bond strengthened as they navigated this new chapter of their lives.

The days that followed were a blur of grief. Jessica and Darwin organized a memorial for Keisha and Amber, inviting all their siblings to attend. It was a somber affair, but it brought a sense of closure to the family. As they shared memories and stories of their lost sisters, they began to feel a sense of peace. The uncertainty and worry that had plagued them for so long were finally laid to rest.

In the weeks that followed, the siblings found themselves growing closer than ever. They leaned on each other for support and comfort, and their bond strengthened as they navigated their grief together. Jessica, in particular, found solace in the company of her brother, Darwin. He had always been her rock, and she was grateful for his unwavering presence by her side.

As time passed, the initial shock and pain began to fade, but the memory of Keisha and Amber remained ever-present in their hearts. Jessica knew that their lives had been challenging and that their endings had been tragic, but she also knew that they had found peace. She took comfort in the thought that her sisters were finally at rest and that their spirits would live on in the love and memories shared by their family.

For Jessica this was just the beginning to a new life for her filled with new family and memories. Jessica and Darwin took some time off from the family search to allow themselves time to let everything that has happened process.

As Jessica and Darwin navigated their grief, they found themselves drawn closer to their remaining siblings. The shared experience of loss and the comfort they offered one another deepened their bonds. Jessica, especially, felt a renewed sense of connection with her brother, Darwin. In the wake of their sisters' deaths, they leaned on each other, sharing memories of Keisha and Amber and finding solace in their shared history.

Jessica's mind often wandered to the lives her sisters had led, the challenges they faced, and the tragic end they met. She wondered about the circumstances that led them to homelessness and the struggles they endured. Despite the sadness that weighed on her heart, she also felt a sense of peace knowing that they were no longer suffering. The uncertainty and worry of their whereabouts had been replaced by a quiet acceptance of their fate.

As time marched on, Jessica and Darwin's grief evolved. The sharp pain of loss softened into a gentle melancholy that they carried with them. They continued to honor their sisters' memories and keep their spirits alive within their hearts. The experience had forever changed them, and they found themselves more appreciative of the family they had found and the love they shared. Jessica, in particular, felt a renewed sense of purpose and gratitude for

the life she was building with her
newfound family.

Dedication

Writing this novel has been a deeply personal journey, and I am profoundly grateful to the many individuals who supported me along the way. First and foremost, I thank my sister for her inspiration to write this book.

Next my family and friends for their unwavering patience and understanding, especially during the challenging periods of research and writing. Their belief in my work sustained me through moments of doubt and self-criticism.

Finally, I extend my gratitude to the countless individuals whose lived experiences have informed this narrative. While the characters and events in this book are fictional, they draw inspiration from the resilience and strength of those who have endured adversity, demonstrating

the remarkable capacity of the
human spirit to heal and find hope
even in the darkest of times.

Author

A. Abney was raised in New England and is the author of several crime and drama books. He draws from his background in law enforcement and psychology to create griping tales that captivates his readers. He also authored his memoir, Divided "A Memoir of a Family I Never Knew", which details his journey through DNA to find his biological family.

www.ingramcontent.com/pod-product-compliance
Lightning Source LLC
Chambersburg PA
CBHW071521100726
47908CB00004B/1252